Erasing All Doubt

Alphas Rule

Doubt Series Book 0.5

Sharon Johnson

Wicked Words Publishing

Published by

Wicked Words Publishing

PO BOX 712

Hamlin, Pa 18427

This book is a work of fiction. While references might be made to actual historical events or existing locations the names, characters, and incidents either are products of the author's imagination or are used fictitiously. Any resemblance to actual persons, living or dead, are entirely coincidental.

The author of this work of fiction acknowledges the trademark status and trademark owners mentioned in this book.

Warning:

This book contains material that may be offensive to some people including graphic language, graphic violence, graphic depictions of death, dubious consent, explicit sex, anal sex, male on male sex, oral sex, rimming, frottage, rough sex, talks of Mpreg, and what may be viewed as BDSM elements.

Author's Note

This work is part of a multi book serial that is not meant to
be read as a stand-alone. Each book will include a new
pairing, but they will all lead to the fulfilling of the
prophecy. This series will be mainly an M/M universe, but
will include episodes that feature different pairings. Future
episodes may include M/M, M/F, M/M/M, M/M/F, F/F. I
promise you by the end every question will be answered
and every bridge will be crossed, but it may not lead you to
where you were expecting.

The greatest obstacle to being heroic is the doubt whether one may not be going to prove one's self a fool; the truest heroism is to resist the doubt; and the profoundest wisdom, to know when it ought to be resisted, and when it be obeyed.

Nathaniel Hawthorne

DEDICATION

I want to thank all the people who've made this book possible. To my loving husband Matthew and our children, I love you more than words could ever express. Without you my life would be empty.

To my editor and friend Pamela, you work tirelessly correcting my mistakes and yet always find the time to raise my spirits. You are so strong and compassionate; you inspire me as not only a writer but as a person.

To Raissa, you know all my levels of crazy and still hang around. Your hard work has made a huge difference and there are no words that can explain all you do for me.

To my assistant and street team, you guys cheer me on and keep me on track, so thank you.

And finally to the readers, who enjoy my stories, seriously, where would I be without you? So thank you to everyone I've mentioned and everyone I've missed, love you. And as always, stay kinky!

Contents

Eighty-six thousand, four hundred seconds. One thousand, four hundred and forty minutes. Twenty-four hours. One day. In his twenty-five years, DeMatteo Santiago had often taken for granted how much could change in a single day.

When DeMatteo crawled into bed at 10:30 p.m. on May 7, 1980, there was no way of knowing how the next twenty-four hours would forever alter his life. As a young Alpha lion shifter, DeMatteo had left his pride in search of his mate and a pride of his own. But the fates had been conspiring for centuries to lead him to this precise moment in time.

May 8, 1980, 10:30 p.m.: a moment in time that will forever change the life of Matthew "DeMatteo" Santiago. Facing the challenges of being the new Alpha of the largest pride in the United States, DeMatteo must find a way to lead in the face of his own personal tragedy.

Prologue

DeMatteo hated visitors in general, but when those visitors came in the middle of the night, DeMatteo's hatred could reach epic levels.

Heavy pounding pulled DeMatteo into consciousness. "This had better be good," DeMatteo growled as he dragged his hand through his mane.

"DeMatteo, open the damn door. It's an emergency!"

Either the words or the panicked tone that they were delivered in pushed DeMatteo's lion fully awake and had him heading to the door before he made a conscious decision to move. As his senses came into focus, the first scent that hit his nostrils was fear, followed quickly by sorrow and blood, lots of blood. His parents' blood.

"What the hell happened?" DeMatteo shouted as he flung open the front door.

"It's your parents, DeMatteo." Paul startled before taking a shaky breath, and this was the first time DeMatteo realized the man was shaking.

A distinct feeling of unease crept up his spine. DeMatteo growled impatiently for the man to continue.

"We were preparing for a hunt... Your parents... Goddammit, you need to just come with me," Paul finally blurted out.

There were few things that could send the normally unflappable man into a complete panic. Putting the clues together, DeMatteo started to feel dizzy.

"Dammit, Paul, just tell me what happened. Are my parents okay?" DeMatteo growled, his voice garbled with his effort to stay human as he felt the predator inside his brain itching to take control.

Paul noticed the Alpha's eyes flickering angry shifter red, forcing him to bare his throat in submission.

"Hunters attacked them as they prepared for the hunt, and they were shot with some kind of poison. The Alpha Mate, she took multiple rounds. She attempted to shield the Alpha with her body. Your mother died within minutes of us reaching them; your father doesn't seem to have much time left. You need to come with me, now!" Paul answered as he turned back towards the tree line.

DeMatteo blindly reached for the spark of his mother through his limited pride bond. Finding nothing but an empty space where her lioness should be, DeMatteo involuntarily shifted.

DeMatteo had only managed to wander some twenty miles from his home pride lands since being forced away from the pride to search for his own lands, but that distance seemed endless as he raced back to what was once his home.

DeMatteo shifted back into his human form mid-stride as he raced into the pride house. DeMatteo followed the scent of blood into the main sitting area where he slid to a halt when he was hit with an overwhelming sickening scent of death and hemlock.

A sob burst from his throat as he saw his mother's lifeless body, her nudity partially covered in respect to her status. Multiple darts could still be seen protruding from her arms and legs, her skin blackened and oozing from the poison that ravaged her system.

Mom? Oh god, please no! DeMatteo thought as his world tilted off its axis. His mother couldn't be dead; she was the strongest lioness DeMatteo had ever seen.

Hearing his father gasping for air pulled his eyes towards his father. His heart thudded painfully as his lion began to roar mournfully in his mind.

"DeMatteo, come here. Paul, as my head enforcer, I need you to be a witness," Matthew rasped, forcing out, "I, Matthew Santiago Sr., do hereby name you, Matthew Santiago Jr., the true Alpha of the Santiago pride."

"W… what are you doing?" DeMatteo asked as he grasped his father's hand. "You're going to make it. We just need a little more time to get an antidote; you just have to hold on," he choked out as all the members of the pride gathered around them to witness the succession of their new Alpha.

"Anyone wishing to challenge him for the position of Alpha, please step forward now." Matthew Sr. spluttered and retched as blood spilled from his lips.

Every member of the pride dropped to their knees and bared their throats as a sign of acceptance of their new Alpha. DeMatteo felt the new stronger pride bond flare to life as each person swore their allegiance to him.

"It is done, son. Take care of your sisters and brother." Matthew Sr. labored for each word, each breath, as the poison ravaged his body from the inside out.

"Please don't leave, Father. I love you," DeMatteo whispered, no sense of hubris able to keep him from begging his dad to fight.

"I have to go, son; my mate is waiting. I love you, all of you." Matthew Sr.'s eyes flickered a weak Alpha red, the last ditch effort of his lion to heal the damage, as he drew his last breath.

DeMatteo roared as he felt his father's life flicker out of the pride. Mournful calls joined his own as the pride wept at the passing of the Alpha and Alpha Mate.

"Alpha, we need to prepare the bodies for burial," Paul whispered, his voice barely audible over the ringing in DeMatteo's ears.

"Have the council Betas see that my parents' bodies are prepared," DeMatteo ordered as he looked at the cubs, though they were not much younger than him, he would now be responsible for caring for them as his own.

The Alpha Pair's cubs never left the pride unless, like DeMatteo, they were born an Alpha. Reaching over to embrace Carla, the youngest of his sisters and the most timid of the cubs, DeMatteo was almost knocked to the floor when all six of his sisters and his one brother, an Omega, clung on to him for comfort.

Taking his siblings upstairs to the main private sitting area, DeMatteo braced himself for a conversation he never expected to have. He just couldn't believe his parents were dead. Shifters were, for the most part, immortal.

DeMatteo had expected to spend the next few years, or decades, as a nomad Alpha male, looking to start his own pride just as his father had done. Now he was the true Alpha, the leader of the most powerful pride in the United States, and parent to his seven siblings.

At only twenty-five, DeMatteo was still a "juvenile Alpha." He hadn't even reached the age where most Alphas found and claimed their true mate, which was an important factor in leading a large pride. Alphas gained considerable power when they mated, especially if they found their true mate. This was important when defending the pride from would-be interlopers.

Although DeMatteo would gain power from each member of his pride, it was small when compared to the power of a true mating. When and if he ever found him, true mates could not start the full bonding process till the Alpha had reached at least the age of thirty-five. That was when he would physically be able to knot his mate and bind them together.

Until then, DeMatteo was burdened with the impossible task of protecting a large territory on his own. He would need to protect and provide for his pride and ensure the continuation of the Santiago blood lines. But as he stared into seven pairs of frightened eyes, DeMatteo knew he had no choice but to succeed.

"Don't worry, little ones. Mom and Dad are together in the summer lands and will watch over us," DeMatteo said with a small smile.

"Will you stay with us tonight, Alpha?" Samantha, the oldest female, asked.

"Of course I will. I'm still just DeMatteo, your big brother, and I will stay as long as you need me." DeMatteo smiled genuinely, as he pulled her into a hug. "I love you, all of you. We will be okay," DeMatteo whispered.

That last part was as much for him as his siblings. The Shifter Council would convene to decide how to deal with the hunters that had killed his parents, and DeMatteo needed to keep his pride safe until then.

Chapter 1

20 years later

"DeMatteo, we are going into town tonight after the gathering. Are you coming?" Samantha asked as she raced into the study.

"No, not tonight. I have to study. I am taking the bar exam next week, and I have to ace it," DeMatteo said without looking up from his book. "Do you have your dress ready for the council gathering tonight?" DeMatteo asked as he finally glanced up. Samantha blushed furiously while staring at the ceiling. DeMatteo sighed, knowing what that look meant.

"You know how important tonight is. You might meet your true mate."

Each Alpha would take an article with the scent markers of any eligible lions back to their pride. These councils normally only happened every one hundred years, though this year's gathering was the exception. After successfully fighting all challenges from rogue Alphas, DeMatteo was being recognized as the true Alpha of the Santiago pride.

Any challenges made now would be considered takeovers and the entire pride could defend their territory. In the upcoming weeks, DeMatteo would also learn the rituals he would be expected to perform as Alpha from the Sages.

"Yes, Alpha. I will go and make sure everyone has their clothing pressed and ready for the gathering," Samantha replied, rolling her eyes.

DeMatteo flashed his eyes at his bratty sister's childish mannerism, which resulted in her baring her throat. He didn't often use his status to subdue his siblings, but sometimes DeMatteo liked to remind them that he could.

As the oldest female, Samantha had often stepped into the role as mother to her younger siblings; it was a role she assumed naturally. Samantha had grown into the mirror image of their mother; standing at five foot ten, she was tall by human standards; but she had an athletic build, long brown mane, and deep brown eyes.

DeMatteo knew his siblings were beautiful and had spent as much time fighting off would be suitors as he had defending his status in the pride. He owed it to his parents to ensure that each of his siblings chose an acceptable mate who would love and treat them well.

DeMatteo knew that at thirty-five his sister would soon be looking for a mate. Only a true mating would allow her to bear cubs; if she took a companion mate she would remain childless until her Alpha was mated. This was one of the many ways the Gods had seen to keeping shifters numbers low and yet another reason for DeMatteo to find his own mate. But seeing as the entire pride raised the cubs, any birth was a blessing shared by all.

Being gay made DeMatteo's chances of finding a true mate more difficult. He had not been able to find one instance of a homosexual Alpha Pair. He had been counseled that if he wanted to continue his family line, he would need to take a female companion mate.

But the Gods had made it that all true mated couples would be able to bear children. They knew it, even though no one in the Santiago pride had ever seen a true mated gay couple. But until his brother was born, there had never been an Omega male in the pride either.

Omegas had always been female and served as the midwives for the pride. But true to Omega heritage,

Timothy was a natural caregiver and was attending college to become a doctor. Mating and breeding were dangerous in the best of situations, so having a doctor, not just a midwife, would be a huge development for the pride.

Two pride members had lost their human true mates during the birth of their cubs due to their need of surgical intervention that was not available. Litters were typically triplets unless the cub was an Alpha or Omega, whose births were always singletons. Mating could be dangerous, especially if not truly mated, if the mating lions were both too dominant and neither lion would submit.

Many first time matings led to the lions nearly tearing each other apart. Even if the mating was successful, bites could require medical assistance. When the mating was with a human, those risks were multiplied. Having a surgeon who knew and understood shifters along with human anatomy would mean better treatment for those injuries and could possibly save lives.

DeMatteo couldn't help the smile that threatened to pull up at his lips as he thought of how proud his parents would be of them and all the changes that had happened within the pride.

DeMatteo finished with his studies just as the first guests began to arrive. He hurried off to the master suite and quickly dressed in the suit his sisters had helped him pick out. When he finally arrived in the main dining room, DeMatteo was not surprised to see that the party was already well under way.

There was a noticeable shift in the mood of the crowd that no doubt announced the arrival of the Alpha Apex and his mate. DeMatteo hurried to the door to welcome their most honored guest and leader of all shifters in North America. As soon as the couple entered, the entire room bared their throats in submission.

"Welcome to the Santiago territories, Alpha and Alpha Mate." DeMatteo made sure to avoid eye contact until he was acknowledged.

"Thank you, Alpha Santiago. Please, everyone, be seated and let's enjoy tonight's festivities," Richard declared.

People milled around with drinks, jockeying to find a seat that allowed them the best view of the presenting of the prior Alpha and Alpha Mate's children. Children from a true Alpha mating were stronger than normal shifters.

Every pride present would jump to take a scent sample back to their home pride.

DeMatteo waited until the room quieted before taking his place on the dais beside the library where his siblings waited to be presented to Greater Shifter Pride Council.

"Greetings. First, I'd like to thank the Alpha Apex and his mate for attending tonight's gala. Next, I'd like to thank the Greater Shifter Pride Council for granting me my father's vacant seat. And finally, I'd like to thank everyone who has traveled to these pride lands to acknowledge my ascension. Now it is my honor to introduce my siblings," DeMatteo began. "Samantha, Julia, and Cassandra: the first litter born to the former Alpha Pair, age thirty-five," DeMatteo announced as the first three girls entered the dining hall.

DeMatteo noticed how all three blushed furiously as they took their places behind him.

"The former Alpha Pair's second litter: Carla, Jenny, and Rebecca, age thirty-two," DeMatteo continued as the second group appeared and also stood behind him.

"And finally my brother, Dr. Timothy Santiago." DeMatteo beamed as his brother quietly entered the room.

DeMatteo frowned as he took in the looks of the other Alphas as they recognized his baby brother's Omega scent. There were looks of surprise, amazement, and more than a few looks of open lust. DeMatteo made a mental note to keep Timothy in his line of sight for the rest of the evening.

"DeMatteo, there is a young shifter coming over from Ireland. His name is Hugh, and he has plans to study here in America. I would consider it a personal favor if you would consider allowing him to join your pride," Richard, the reigning Alpha Apex, stated as they conversed inside DeMatteo's office.

"As you know, Alpha, we are always looking to expand the pride with more breeding males. Any male you recommend would be well-received," DeMatteo replied.

"Very good. He is scheduled to arrive in America in two weeks' time. Would you be able to have someone there to ensure his entrance through customs?"

"Of course, Alpha."

After spending a few minutes learning about Hugh's pride status, DeMatteo was given a cache of documents they would need for immigration. Shaking DeMatteo's hand before taking his leave, Richard left the office and made his way over to the group of shifters who had gathered by the fireplace.

Tonight the entire Santiago pride would have a run with the Alpha Apex and the visiting Alphas, and DeMatteo knew he would have to keep an eye on his brother. Spotting him alone by the stairs, DeMatteo decided it was best to let him know the dangers he would be facing.

"Timothy, tonight during the pride run, I need you to stay in the center of the pride," DeMatteo whispered low enough that only his brother could hear.

"Yes, DeMatteo. Even though we are sticking to pride lands, where I can guarantee I will not get lost or distracted, even as an Omega," Timothy stated, only slightly annoyed at the implications.

"Timothy, you know that is not what I meant. Why do you insist on making everything so difficult? Is it that hard to believe that this is just me, your older brother, looking out for your safety?" DeMatteo asked, glancing around.

"Let's continue this in private."

Taking Timothy by the arm, DeMatteo lead him to the upstairs office, knowing his enforcers would stop anyone trying to follow.

"Most of these Alphas do not have Omegas in their pride. They will do anything to have one."

Placing his hand on Timothy's nape, DeMatteo continued, "Having the Alpha Apex here will provide some protection, but as your Alpha and more importantly as your brother, it is my job to protect you."

Timothy pressed into his hand, purring at the affection his brother so readily provided. As an Omega, Timothy naturally sought out his Alpha's approval. Their natural roles as protector and healer balanced together to create a more stable healthy pride.

"Okay, DeMatteo. I'm sorry I snapped at you; it's just all these strange lions have me nervous. I will be sure to stay in the center of the pride. In case I haven't said it lately, thank you."

Timothy had always looked to his brother for comfort and protection as a cub and he still basked in the love DeMatteo openly displayed.

"There's no need to thank me. I love you."

Later that evening...

Five hundred shifters gathered into one place would be too much temptation for human hunters or other shifter clans looking to cause trouble. The fact that the Alpha Apex and his mate were present made the risk of an attack too great to be ignored.

One hundred and fifty of the best hunters in the pride were set up as sentinels around the forest, along with fifty other volunteers. They would patrol the grounds, as well as man tree top observation posts.

Conversations continued as lions young and old stripped in preparation for the run. DeMatteo struggled to keep his eye on Timothy through the crowds as the laughing and celebrations continued. He was startled when Timothy appeared at his side with two of the Alpha Apex's personal guards.

"Looks like everyone will be watching out for me tonight."

DeMatteo's response was stilled when the Alpha Apex shifted and let out a roar for all to follow. His own lion all but ripped through the change, eager to join their

Alpha in a hunt. One by one, each lion shifted in submission and gathered around their leader.

The Alpha Apex lifted his head and released a roar that shook the trees and alerted all the lions for miles around that it was time to hunt.

After a twenty mile run, and many successful kills, the majority of the visiting Alphas headed back to their temporary lodging in and around the Santiago pride lands.

"Alpha, I would like to thank you for your blessings and all the help you gave me since I became leader," DeMatteo said as he walked Richard to his car.

"DeMatteo, you know I loved my brother. He would be so proud of you. As I am, I love you."

"Thank you, Uncle Richard. I love you too," DeMatteo replied, wary of the other shifters who might've been listening.

Most of the prides knew that the Alpha Apex was related to DeMatteo, but they never showed any familiar attachments at formal events so DeMatteo was slightly surprised by this public display of affection.

He hadn't realized until now how much he wanted Richard's approval. Being the youngest group of his father's children, and the only offspring of the Alpha's true mate, DeMatteo and his siblings had struggled to ensure that none of his thirty other half siblings felt slighted.

Their mother had always loved his half-brothers and sisters like her own. His father had sired many cubs before meeting his true mate, so having his uncle say he had done well lifted a burden DeMatteo never knew he was carrying.

Chapter 2

"Alpha Santiago. This is Alpha Sterling. One of the scent markers I received at the gathering appears to have a mate in my pride."

"Really. That is fantastic news." DeMatteo's lion bristled at the idea of losing a pride member.

But deciding which lion changed prides generally depended on which lion was most dominant. Binary concepts such as male or female did not play a large role. The more submissive partner followed the most dominant, and there were few exceptions.

"Yes, Alpha, I thought so as well. I was phoning to make an official request to return to your territory with my Beta to confirm this true mate match."

"Yes, of course. And any discussions of moving can be decided at that time."

"Does two days from now work for you?"

"Yes, that is doable. Giving them the weekend to begin bonding."

"I look forward to seeing you again and strengthening our pride's connection with a true mate bonding."

"Likewise, Alpha Sterling," DeMatteo conceded.

Ending the call, DeMatteo was amazed at the many changes his pride would be expecting in the new days. As of that moment, he was still waiting for his four betas to return with the newest member of the Pride: Hugh Lucas McKinney, age twenty-six, relocating from Ireland to go to school for architecture. DeMatteo had gone over all of the information his uncle had provided. Still, there had to be something that was left out. Surely there were plenty of good schools in Ireland. Why travel to America, let alone Seattle, for that?

Whatever it was, DeMatteo was sure he would get all the answers he needed when Hugh arrived. Any chance of meeting with a new male lion was also a possible mate match. DeMatteo refused to get his hopes up, but the fates had a way of guiding mates together.

You just have to be open to their gentle persuasions, his lion stated. And with the news he had just received of a potential true mate match within the pride, DeMatteo had even more reasons to be hopeful.

"Alpha. Hugh has arrived. Would you like to speak with him now or have him shown to his quarters?" Samantha asked as she flopped down on the office couch.

"Don't you knock before entering your Alpha's office?" DeMatteo asked, but the hint of humor in his voice took all the bite out of the question.

"Send him in and tell Timothy to get the mating ritual area prepared for a true mating. No. Before you ask, I will tell you about it tonight when I tell everyone else. Now get out of my office."

To say his meeting with Hugh was unexpected was putting it mildly. To think that there were still prides that committed such abuses was abhorrent. Now that Timothy had taken their newest pride member to his room, DeMatteo would take action.

"Hello, Uncle. Hugh has arrived safely but the story he has told me is much more than just seeking an education. According to Hugh, he was in fact sent away forcibly by his former Alpha. The incidents he described leads me to believe that there may be some serious crimes being committed in the Malory pride."

The fact that DeMatteo greeted him as a family member and not a submissive Alpha immediately caught Richard's attention. Only the most urgent matters brushed away his sense of formalities.

"I see. Do you have any evidence to bring forward to the Council?"

DeMatteo let out an annoyed huff, as therein lay the real problem. He wanted his uncle to start a formal investigation with no more than one shifter's accusation. The Council dictated that each continent be governed by an Alpha Apex, whose duty it was to protect all shifters inside of their jurisdiction.

It was almost unheard of for an outside Alpha Apex and Council to investigate charges of abuse or neglect without substantial evidence to support their claim. To falsely accuse an Alpha Apex, and by proxy his Council, of crimes could be seen as an act of war.

"I don't have any to offer except Hugh's statement."

"Start from the beginning; tell me everything."

"While the incidents you describe are truly reprehensible, I don't think that there is much I can do without any kind of proof. The council will never risk starting a war with only one shifter's word against that of his former Alpha, who also happens to be the Apex of that area."

"Do you think Tien would be able to get enough evidence to convince the Council of the crimes committed? She could compel the Alpha and his children to confess what really caused them to send him away."

"Perhaps, but the Alpha would have to submit to the ritual. We have no grounds to demand it, and even the request could be seen as a move towards judgement."

"Dammit. There has to be something we can do. There are laws in place that protect weaker shifters. Maybe if I contact him directly with some questions regarding Hugh's breakdown, I could get him to at least agree to punish his daughter for her crimes."

"DeMatteo, your heart is in the right place, but I don't think…" Richard paused.

"What? You don't think what?" DeMatteo blurted out.

"There may be another way to find out what really happened and get evidence of any crime that was committed."

Richard paused, and DeMatteo could hear him consulting his mate on whatever new plan he had devised. They spoke in hushed whispers that even with his heightened senses DeMatteo couldn't make out, no doubt the results of Tien's magic, before Richard continued.

"I could speak to my contact Henry on the Hunter's Council. Off the record - of course - let him know I have a tip of a shifter that is going against the treaty. Let them investigate and bring charges. They are free to investigate with little evidence, and if they find nothing, we will have our answers."

"That is perfect. How soon do you think they can get started?"

"Now DeMatteo, I'm not making you any promises. But I know they'll take this allegation seriously. I will call my contact tomorrow and keep you posted."

"Thank you, Uncle. I really appreciate you doing this for me."

"Don't thank me yet."

DeMatteo hung up the phone and stared at the ordinary-looking file his uncle had given him on Hugh before his arrival. After reading it over two more times, DeMatteo was finally satisfied that there were no clues he had somehow overlooked. The only thing he could do was hope that his uncle's contact could uncover the truth.

"You wanted to see me?" Timothy asked as he walked into his Alpha's private office. DeMatteo was seated behind his desk, papers and books covering every square inch of space and stacked high on the couches.

"Yes, Timothy. Take a seat. I meant to speak to you yesterday, but after everything with Hugh..." DeMatteo sighed as he rubbed the bridge of his nose.

Timothy glanced around the room at the various stacks of books and papers leaning precariously against every surface and decided to remain standing. DeMatteo chuckled as he too glanced around the cluttered space before shrugging.

"Well, as you can see, everything went to shit. But that is not why I wanted to see you. I have great news for you, little brother. It seems as though you may have found your true mate!"

Timothy blinked a few times as he realized what his brother was saying. Suddenly, he felt the need to sit down as his lion leapt around and chased its tail excitedly in his mind. "You're serious?" Timothy asked cautiously.

"Completely. Her name is Kimberly Atkins, and she should be traveling up with her Alpha within the next few days," DeMatteo announced, pleased that he was able to give his brother the news most shifters waited decades to hear.

Chapter 3

Hugh ~

Hugh couldn't believe how lucky he was to be accepted into the Santiago pride. At first, he thought he was being punished for being a bad companion, but the longer he stayed here, the more he believed that maybe his old Alpha had been trying to help when he sent him away.

It had been difficult to tell DeMatteo why he had been sent to America, and he still felt the heat rush to his face when he had to relive his shame.

"So, Hugh. Tell me why you chose to leave your birth pride and travel to America."

Although he had known this question would be asked, he had still hoped to spend a few days in the pride before the Alpha judged his worthiness.

"Uhm…" Hugh fidgeted and tried to decide the best way to tell his new Alpha that his companion had sent him away for being gay.

"Well, my companion no longer wanted me, and someone had to leave so…" he finished lamely.

"Wait. Why would you have to leave because of a breakup?"

Hugh felt nauseated. He couldn't lie to the Alpha, who obviously was not going to accept a partial story. Maybe he already knew, and this was some kind of test to see if he was a liar on top of being a deviant.

"Well, Alpha, my companion mate was one of the daughters of the Alpha, and I had been promised to her since childhood. But once she learned I was unable to satisfy her as a companion, she decided to punish me before making me leave the pride."

He could tell that his new Alpha didn't know what to do with the information he was receiving. It wasn't as if Hugh could lie even if he wanted to, even if lying would save him from whatever punishment he would receive for being a deviant. Hugh tried to remain passive, to present a smaller target for the larger shifter's wrath, but his body began to tremble uncontrollably.

"I told her I was gay after I was unable to perform sexually. She forced me to orally perform for her brothers and friends. Since I couldn't satisfy her, I could be used as a form of currency."

Hugh could no longer stop the tears as he remembered being forced to his knees while males he had once thought of as friends forced their cocks down his throat, not stopping even as he cried and begged for mercy or while he choked or gagged during the brutal assault.

"Someone alerted the Alpha of my mistreatment, and he made arrangements for me to leave the pride."

Hugh immediately bared his throat as the Alpha stalked over to him, bracing himself for the inevitable attack. He was not prepared for the Alpha lion to pull him into his arms and gently stroke his back while whispering nonsensical words meant to comfort.

"Okay. Hugh. It's over now; you're safe here."

Hugh was completely out of his element. He had no idea how to deal with this. He was expecting, even accepting, any and all violence others chose to give him, but this was something new and confusing to both him and his lion.

He wanted to pull away, but he feared any sign of refusal to submit would be met with unspeakable violence. Even though the touch conveyed kindness, Hugh was sure that this was a new way to torture him. Maybe if he offered himself willingly, this Alpha would keep him as a personal pet.

"Tim, I need you to come to my office immediately..." Hugh could hear the Alpha speaking even as his lion began to take over more of his mind. He could feel his body shaking as he began to shift.

"It's okay, Hugh, Timothy is my brother and the pride Omega. He is also our doctor and will be able to get you settled into your room." Hugh's lion flicked its ears as the Alpha began to gently pet his fur. Although he still felt threatened, the lion wanted desperately to be accepted by this Alpha.

Hugh calmed some with this; his lion felt more comfortable with an Omega in the room. Their very purpose was to care and nurture, and they were completely incapable of hurting others.

Pushing those painful memories away, Hugh focused back on his school work. That had been seven months ago, and since then his life had gotten better every day. But that was also the day that Hugh had decided he was completely in love with his handsome Alpha.

After Timothy arrived in DeMatteo's office, he had calmed Hugh and taken him into what would become his room in the pride house. Being around an Omega made Hugh and his lion feel at ease, as this was the only person he knew without a doubt would never hurt him.

After a physical, Timothy gave him a tranquilizer often used on big cats to help him get some sleep. Before he drifted off, Hugh could hear a furious DeMatteo yelling at who Hugh would later learn was the Alpha Apex, and DeMatteo had demanded that an investigation be conducted on his former pride.

Never before had anyone fought to protect him. Not even his parents had fought against letting him be promised to a woman forty years his senior. Not even when he confessed to being gay did they try to stop the doomed mating.

They had been taught that being gay was unnatural for shifters and that was why gay shifters never found their true mates. Hugh drifted off to sleep with the knowledge that the fates had sent him to be with his mate. The one person who would always protect and care for him.

Hugh ~ Two years later...

After suffering for years in his former pride, Hugh had found himself where he always wanted to be. He was at the top of his class, well on his way to graduating with honors, and he was in a serious, healthy relationship with his Alpha. DeMatteo had been the perfect companion, and though they had yet to consummate their bond, Hugh knew that the Alpha cared deeply for him.

"Hugh, where are you?"

The sound of DeMatteo's younger sister, Samantha, pulled him out of his musings. Since joining the pride, there had only been one person that Hugh had viewed somewhat as a foe, and that was Samantha. At first, it had been because she'd treated him like a pathetic victim.

After the Alpha Apex started his informal investigation, he'd quickly gathered enough information to level several complaints against the pride and Alpha. Once the news spread and everyone was made aware of Hugh's shame, people began to look at him with open pity.

After convincing everyone he was fine, while in truth he was far from it, most people just went back to their normal lives. But not Samantha, who seemed to watch his every move. Especially since he started dating the Alpha.

"Hugh, didn't I tell you that everyone needed to be out for Timothy's mating ceremony?"

"Yes, but I have to finish my homework, and I have a date with DeMatteo tomorrow." Hugh barely suppressed the growl in his throat.

"You have five minutes to get your ass to the gathering!" Samantha roared, causing the smaller shifter to bare his throat.

Satisfied with his submission, she stalked to his door, almost ripping it from its hinges. At the last minute she turned and faced Hugh.

"It'd be best if you remember your place. I am the second in command. You are not the Alpha's mate. You are not even acknowledged as his chosen companion. You will follow the hierarchy. My brother cares for you, but he is an honorable Alpha and will not tolerate you disobeying pride code."

Hugh bared his teeth at the slammed door before gathering his things to head to the clearing. It made no sense that he was required to attend; it wasn't as if any of the Santiago siblings gave a shit about him.

They all looked at him as some sort of placeholder until the Alpha met his "true" mate even though Hugh knew that gay shifters did not have mates. They were an abomination to the Gods, so it was easy to convince both DeMatteo and his siblings that he would step aside when the time came.

But Hugh would never move over for someone to steal his mate. He would fight to the death to protect, and keep, the mate he had chosen for himself. He just needed enough time to show DeMatteo that he could be the perfect mate.

Hugh would erase all doubt DeMatteo had about them being destined to be together. He just needed enough time to show them all.

"So, Timothy, are you ready to finally complete the bond?" DeMatteo asked as they stood in front of the altar waiting for the mating ceremony to begin.

"You have no idea; I wish that we could skip the ceremony altogether."

"You know you were right to hold off, right? Not many shifters would have been able to wait so long after exchanging a mating bite to fully claim their mate."

"Yeah, but Kimberly needed to complete college before moving cross country. It hasn't been easy, but I wanted to make her happy."

"You're a good man, Timothy. Better than me. I think my lion would have hunted her down."

"Well, I'm not sure that is completely off the table. I might need you to command me not to mount her right here on the dais."

DeMatteo's eyes widened as he realized how serious his brother was about the possibility of a shift. His eyes blazed Alpha red as his lion came forward. "You will not shift. You will maintain control until you take your mate to your den after the ceremony. Do you understand me?"

Timothy's eyes glowed yellow in response to his Alpha's command. "Yes, Alpha. Thank you, Alpha."

"Don't mention it," DeMatteo said. The room was silent as the Mage took his place, signaling the beginning of the bonding ceremony.

They both watched as Kimberly was escorted by her father down the aisle. DeMatteo took a step back as the bride-to-be stood beside her true mate. DeMatteo couldn't help but wonder who would one day stand beside him as the Mage began the ceremony.

"Though we are unable to give all this knowledge to these two who stand before us, we can hope to leave with them the knowledge of love and its strengths and the anticipation of the wisdom that comes with time. The law of life is love unto all beings. Without love, life is nothing; without love, death has no redemption. Love is anterior to Life, posterior to Death, initial of Creation, and the exponent of Earth. If we learn no more in life, let it be this: to love."

DeMatteo was struck by how happy his baby brother was, and while he was overjoyed with Timothy's mating, he couldn't help but feel a pang of wanting. His lion grew more impatient with every passing day. He decided, right there in the middle of the vows, to double the search for his true mate.

"Marriage is a bond to be entered into only after considerable thought and reflection. As with any aspect of life, it has its cycles, its ups and its downs, its trials and its triumphs. With full understanding of this, this man and woman have come here today to be joined as one in marriage. Others would ask at this time who gives away the bride in marriage, but as no person is property to be bought and sold, given and taken, I ask simply if she comes of her own will and if she has her family's blessing…"

Chapter 4

"Alpha, may I speak with you?" Carla asked as she stood outside DeMatteo's door.

Normally, he enjoyed getting visits from his siblings at his office. But the formal request for an audience made his lion perk up. None of his siblings ever addressed DeMatteo by his title unless they needed something outside his role of brother.

"Of course, Carla. Please close the door and have a seat."

DeMatteo could tell before she entered the room that Carla was upset by the fear-laced scent that wafted in with her. His own lion became increasingly aggravated by the distress signals her lioness was projecting. He waited until she was seated before pressing her for details.

"Okay, so what is wrong? Is it that human you have been courting?"

"Yes," Carla stammered. Her eyes bulged at DeMatteo's low growl. "I mean, not in a bad way. It's just that I want to tell him the truth about me and ask him to be my companion mate," Carla blurted quickly, trying to calm her Alpha before he hunted her boyfriend down like the human was a rabid dog.

DeMatteo deflated as he realized that Carla was asking permission to mate, not seeking her brother's protection from a bad guy. Even though he had always known this day would come, he had hoped that all his siblings wouldn't meet their mates so soon.

"Is that so? You have only been together a year; do you think he would agree to mating?" DeMatteo questioned.

"Yes. To all of it, yes. I know he loves me, and I think once you explain everything, he will accept," Carla explained.

DeMatteo was just about to agree when he realized what his sister was asking him to do. "Me? Why do you need me to explain it?"

"Please, DeMatteo! I know he will accept, but that chance that he won't has my lion so agitated I am afraid I might shift in the middle of the talk. I can't risk losing him!"

"Goddammit, Carla," DeMatteo growled. Each lion was expected to stand before the Council and petition for their human companion mate's acceptance into a pride. And the thought of talking to the human had DeMatteo's lion pacing.

"I will speak with the Council on your behalf. And if—" DeMatteo started.

"Thank you!" Carla cut him off and jumped out of her chair to hug DeMatteo.

DeMatteo tried to pry off the overexcited cub before she completely ruined his speech. "Don't thank me yet. If they accept him, Timothy and I will need you to bring him to the pride lands so I can bring him into the 'know.'" DeMatteo finished.

DeMatteo laughed out loud when Carla proceeded to do some of the most ridiculous dance moves he'd ever seen around his office. His laugh cut off when Carla hugged him tight.

"Thank you so much, DeMatteo! You are the best brother and Alpha!" Carla exclaimed.

"I already said yes; you can stop sucking up now," DeMatteo joked as he pushed her away again. "Okay, okay. Get out of here, Carla, before I change my mind."

"Seriously, DeMatteo, thank you," Carla said as she grabbed her purse that had fallen on the floor during her celebrations.

"You're welcome, kid."

"Love you," Carla said as she headed to the door.

"Love you, too."

DeMatteo waited until he heard her getting on the elevators before he called the Alpha Apex office.

"Greetings, Uncle Richard."

"Hello, DeMatteo, it's been too long. To what do I owe the honor of this call?" Richard greeted. Shame welled up in him as he thought that it might have been months before he called if he hadn't needed his Uncle to set up this meeting.

"It has. We really need to get together for dinner. The cubs in the pride would love to see you and Tien," DeMatteo conceded. It had been months since he had seen his Uncle, as the number of clients he saw daily kept him busy most days and all his free time was spent courting Hugh.

"That is a wonderful idea! I will check with your aunt and come up with a date," Richard agreed easily.

"Fantastic, but there is another official reason for my call."

"I was afraid of that. What can I do for you?" Richard questioned.

DeMatteo couldn't blame his uncle for his suspicions; the last time he had called requesting a favor, it had almost caused an international incident.

"Relax, Uncle Richard. This is good news. I need to request a hearing with the Council. Carla has requested to seek approval of a companion mate," DeMatteo said.

"Wow! That is exciting news. Your Aunt Tien will be thrilled. Let me call the Council. Nephew, tell Carla that Tien and I send our love."

"I will. You can reach me in the office. I'll be here for at least five more hours."

"Perfect. It shouldn't take longer than an hour or two. The Council is always eager to hear mating petitions."

"Thanks, Uncle Richard," DeMatteo said as he ended the call.

DeMatteo stared out his office window, deep in thought, after the call ended. He hadn't been before the Council since they had met to administer the fate of the hunters who had killed his parents. Within days of their deaths, the Hunter's Council had turned over Stephen and Vivian Mitchell for the murder of his parents.

They were tried by a joint commission of human and shifter elders, and the evidence presented by the lead investigator Henry Steinbeck ensured a unanimous decision: guilty on all charges, with the penalty of death.

"DeMatteo, the commission has spoken, but you do not have to be the one to carry out their sentence," Tien said as she carefully watched his face.

She had erected a privacy field around them after the committee had made their decision. He had to decide if he would carry out the prisoners' executions personally or if he wanted the committee's enforcers to carry out the task.

It was strange to be able to see the Council and the people that murdered his parents and know that they could not hear or see anything that was happening right in front of them. DeMatteo was amazed every time he got to witness just how powerful his aunt really was.

"I know, Aunt Tien, but I need to do it. Not out of some sense of revenge, but as the Alpha of the Santiago pride, it is my duty to see that my pride is paid recompense for the loss of the Alpha Pair," DeMatteo said as he stripped.

Tien smiled like that was the correct answer as she grabbed a robe to cover his nudity. DeMatteo loved his aunt, but she always seemed to answer in riddles, leaving him with few answers and even more questions.

"Yes, DeMatteo, I believe you will make a fine Alpha indeed. It has been written that you will do great things."

"Thank you?" DeMatteo answered, although it came out more like a question.

"Don't worry, my sweet nephew; these things will make sense in time," Tien stated cryptically.

The Alpha Apex approached the pair, and Tien allowed him into the shield. Richard approached DeMatteo, and right then they were not uncle and nephew. This was the Alpha Apex of North America addressing a lesser Alpha.

"Alpha Santiago."

"Yes, Alpha Apex," DeMatteo answered respectfully.

"The committee requires your decision."

"I will carry out the sentences for the Santiago pride," DeMatteo said without hesitation, certain that this was what his parents would have wanted him to do.

"Very well," Richard stated. He nodded to Tien, who lowered the shield and allowed the others in the room to hear and see them.

"Will the condemned please rise," Richard commanded.

The hunters sneered in contempt, attempting to ignore the order, and remained seated. They were snatched from their seats by the wolf shifters who traditionally held the role as neutral enforcers for interspecies committees, their faces shifted as they bared their teeth in threat.

"For the murder of Alpha Mate Sabrina and Alpha Matteo Santiago, you are hereby condemned to death, and your family is banned from holding positions within the hunter council. Are there any last messages or apologies you wish to make before the sentence is carried out?" Richard continued, unfazed by the hunter's disrespect.

"No," Stephen ground out as he boldly stared into the eyes of the Alpha Apex.

"Yes, there is. I would like it to be noted that you are siding with these animals over hunters that have served humanity for generations. Do not think your treachery will not be paid back in kind," Vivian said.

It was obvious to all present that neither hunter felt any remorse for what they had done. The Human Council had been shocked when they had learned of the Mitchell family's involvement in the Alpha Pair murders. Shock had quickly given way to disgust as the duo had bragged when questioned. They had actually taken their small granddaughter to witness their crime.

The vote was unanimous to turn them over to the Shifter Council; not to do so would constitute an act of war between the species. The only dissent had been made by Henry Steinbeck, as their families had a long history of collaboration. His main concern had been that if the entire family was excommunicated, their child would be made an orphan if the shifters demanded recompense. Hunter families were matriarchal, and he did not believe that Chris would be able to raise his next leader without guidance.

"Very well; it is noted. Scribe, let it also be said that even in the face of their own demise, Mr. and Mrs. Mitchell have continued to bring disgrace to the hunter's code. Alpha Matthew Santiago, it has been decided that Stephen and Vivian have committed grave crimes against the whole of the Santiago pride and have broken the human and shifter treaty. For their unsolicited and unsanctioned

murder of the former Alpha Pair, illegal and unsupervised cultivation of poison designed specifically to attack shifters, and trespass on protected pride land, their lives are forfeit. It is the understanding of the committee that you as the current Alpha of the Santiago pride seek your due recompense," Reynold Jackowitz, head of the Human Council, said.

"Yes," DeMatteo answered.

His lion was furious just beneath the surface. It took all his control to follow protocol and not just kill them now. The entire trial had been a practice in patience, and only Samantha had remained with him during the proceedings. DeMatteo looked to the back of the room and noticed that all his siblings had chosen to be present for the sentencing and execution.

"So let it be noted. Let us bear witness to the fulfillment of the order," Reynold and Richard commanded in unison.

Finally allowed to dispense final judgement, DeMatteo wasted no time. He dropped his robe and shifted into his lion.

Stephen's screams were cut off as DeMatteo leapt, going straight for the throat; blood sprayed across the female huntress's back as she attempted to run. Tien had anticipated the move and had already placed a barrier around the group.

It took seconds for Vivian to realize that she was trapped. DeMatteo's lion relished in the stench of fear that washed over him as he stalked his prey. This was the monster that had killed his parents, and his lion wanted to bathe in their blood for hurting the pride. Her death was much slower as DeMatteo pulled her apart, limb by limb.

Tien lowered the barrier as DeMatteo walked over to each hunter and urinated on their remains. It was the ultimate disgrace to be torn apart and pissed on, showing the lion's hatred for the prey it had killed.

As DeMatteo returned to human form, he was approached by the human investigator.

"I am sorry for your loss, Alpha Santiago. Please know that if we had known what they had planned, the entire Council would have stepped in."

"Thank you, Henry. The Santiago pride holds no ill will towards the Human Council; recompense has been

paid in full, " DeMatteo said as he wiped the larger pieces of gore from his body.

DeMatteo had walked away that night with a vow that he would have very limited contact with humans. But now his baby sister was seeking to take a human as a companion mate and asking him to stand in front of the committee in her stead.

DeMatteo ran his hands through his hair as he waited for his Uncle to call with the Council's decision. He would need to speak with Timothy to arrange a meeting with Nick if he passed the Council's vetting process.

Chapter 5

DeMatteo ~ Six months later...

"DeMatteo, tell me again why I have to keep my eyes closed?" Hugh stumbled slightly as they moved up the staircase, groping around like he was trying to get an idea of where they were headed.

DeMatteo swatted his hands away, taking him by the wrist and leading him down the darkened corridor towards the master bedroom. They had been taking things slow over the last several months, DeMatteo ever cautious of Hugh's past, and he didn't want the other man to feel rushed or pressured.

The other reason was because DeMatteo's lion was indifferent of the shifter as a companion. He saw him as a pride member, but this was not their true mate so it paid to be cautious and allow both lions to grow accustomed to the other's proximity. After lots of exploration, they had decided tonight would be the time they would have anal sex for the first time.

"I'm going to need you to trust me. Can you do that for me, baby?" DeMatteo asked as they entered the room.

Hugh trembled slightly as the door closed behind him. DeMatteo responded by crowding him back against the wall, his arms bracketing the smaller man. Slowly DeMatteo's thumb lightly traced a path from Hugh's ear to his chin.

"May I kiss you?" DeMatteo asked, as his thumb caressed Hugh's full bottom lip.

Hugh ~

Hugh was unable to speak over the roaring of blood in his ears, but he managed a slight nod before DeMatteo pressed their lips together. Hugh knew there was little chance of either of them finding their true mate; being gay was a rare abnormality in the shifter world. But this, here with his Alpha, was good and Hugh refused to let his past ruin this chance to be happy.

The kiss began chaste, a simple press of lips as the Alpha caressed their flesh together. As Hugh began to relax in his embrace, DeMatteo peppered his mouth with light kisses before licking the seams, begging for admittance.

"Let me in, little cub," DeMatteo chuffed. Hugh couldn't help the way his body trembled in DeMatteo's arms at the affectionate term.

Hugh's mouth opened eagerly when his Alpha nibbled on his bottom lip. Hugh felt his lion roll belly up in submission, wanting to please their alpha.

Slipping in his tongue, DeMatteo all but swallowed each of Hugh's moan as he mapped out his mouth. When Hugh licked the roof of his mouth DeMatteo groaned deep in his throat.

Hugh thrusted his hips eagerly when DeMatteo slipped his hands around his waist, and pulled Hugh flush against him. He moaned out in appreciation when DeMatteo wedged a thigh between his legs.

Hugh tentatively reached up to stroke DeMatteo's hair as he deepened the kiss while grinding his aching cock against DeMatteo.

DeMatteo broke the kiss right when breathing became necessary and pulled off Hugh's shirt. Placing a soft kiss on his lips, he then began his journey across his chin and down his neck. He nipped every so often, soothing the abused flesh with his tongue and Hugh would be embarrassed by the whorish sounds he made if he could get his brain to care.

DeMatteo ~

DeMatteo ran his tongue across the well-defined pecs and across Hugh's already pebbled nipple. He allowed his fangs to drop and graze the raised nub before blowing air across the object of his abuse.

"Ah, please, Alpha," Hugh gasped as DeMatteo pulled the nub between his lips and sucked.

"That's it, cub. Take what you need." DeMatteo gripped his hips tighter encouraging Hugh to speed up his frantic thrusts. DeMatteo reached between their writhing bodies to pop Hugh's button and lower his zipper. He stepped back after he gave Hugh's bottom lip a good nip. He dropped to his knees and dragged Hugh's pants and boxers down in one swift motion.

"Oh my god," Hugh gasped, his entire body trembling and DeMatteo could almost taste the lust as it buzzed through his body.

DeMatteo flicked his tongue across the crown and dipped into his slit while he removed Hugh's pants. DeMatteo stood back up and swiftly pressed their lips together before he directed Hugh towards the bed.

Hugh's body tensed when DeMatteo led him towards the bed. While DeMatteo rationally knew that Hugh was there of his own free will and that as his Alpha DeMatteo would never harm him, it was obvious that the sexual abuse he had suffered at the hands of his old pride caused the bitter scent of fear rolling off him.

"Are you okay, baby?" DeMatteo asked. "You know we do not have to do anything?"

Hugh visibly tried to shake the past from his head and slowly blinked, he suddenly looked terrified that his hesitation would somehow upset his Alpha.

"No! I want to do this," Hugh rushed out.

DeMatteo could see where the tears threatened to spill and that was enough to almost make DeMatteo give up. Hugh needed this to be good; and DeMatteo needed to make this good for his young lover. "I'm just… That was my first real kiss. I don't know what to do," Hugh confessed.

The last part came out a mere whisper, so soft DeMatteo would have missed it if not for his lion's hearing. He didn't want any of the demons from Hugh's past in this bed. Hugh may not be his true mate, but DeMatteo truly cared for him and wanted to make this experience perfect.

"That's okay, baby. I will take care of you," DeMatteo said as he cupped Hugh's jaw. He ignored all the warning bells in his head telling him that Hugh might not be as ready as he said. "Lie down, baby. I need to get you ready."

Hugh immediately laid on his back and opened his legs, and DeMatteo was presented with such a blatant invitation that even his lion acknowledged the man beneath them. Renewed lust crawled into his belly, but DeMatteo pushed it down, determined to be gentle.

His own pants were removed, and DeMatteo settled between Hugh's thighs before he placed a gentle kiss on his stomach. DeMatteo reached into the drawer to retrieve the oil he kept for his occasional bed partners, and DeMatteo made sure to graze Hugh's dick with his abs.

DeMatteo licked a path from root to tip, and poured a copious amount of lube into his palm. He licked across his slit and scooped up the pearl of pre-come that had accumulated there.

"Oh. My. God!" Hugh gasped, the sheets clutched tight in his fist.

"That's it, just relax. You are going to love this," DeMatteo said before he slipped the tip between his lips while he circled the tight rosebud he was about to defile. DeMatteo continued to slowly circle his fingers when he felt the slight flutter of the stubborn muscles that surrendered to his ministrations.

"Open up, little cub," he chuffed as he slowly pushed in to the second knuckle. After a few seconds, DeMatteo began to pull and stretch out the delicate tissue before he slid in a second finger.

"Please... Oh god." Hugh felt the sweat on his brow as he squirmed on the thick digit that invaded him. Suddenly that digit became a duo and as the pain became unbearable, those fingers curled and touched the bundle of nerves that sent a blast of pleasure up his spine.

"There you go, baby," DeMatteo chuffed as he continued to massage that walnut-sized gland.

"Remember this feeling, Hugh. This is what makes it worth the pain."

DeMatteo slowly scissored his fingers and kept the pressure steady until he felt Hugh's muscles relax before his fingers were sucked back in. A third finger was inserted and he took the opportunity to pour some oil directly in his hole, DeMatteo making sure every inch was completely coated.

Hugh ~

Hugh was amazed as the pressure and pain morphed into the greatest pleasure he had ever experienced. Nothing had felt this good, not fucking a woman, not stroking his cock. No one had ever made lights dance behind his eyes and his legs tremble. No one had ever cared to make sure he was enjoying what they were doing to him.

As DeMatteo continued to hit that spot without fail, Hugh couldn't help but roll his hips into the sensation. As the tempo increased and the pleasure grew, Hugh shamelessly rode those fingers, seeking his orgasm that remained just out of reach.

"Please… DeMatteo …." Hugh begged, although he had no idea what he was begging for. "More…oh god… I need more."

DeMatteo gently removed his fingers before he helped Hugh roll onto his belly. Even with his shifter healing there would be some pain, of course there would, but DeMatteo seemed determined to make this one thing Hugh would never regret. A gentle tug urged Hugh onto his hands and knees.

"Okay," Hugh whimpered as he maneuvered into position.

"This is better for the first time," DeMatteo whispered as he pulled Hugh's hips further back. There was some crinkling noise which Hugh imagined was a condom being opened, and then there was an insistent pressure against his hole, huge and slick with oil, causing Hugh to tense up slightly.

DeMatteo patiently waited for him to relax, stroking gently down his sides while he kept up a continuous stream of words of encouragement.

Hugh ~

Hugh struggled to let his body unclench, partly nervous and partly disappointed that DeMatteo had chosen not to form a true companion bond with him by wearing a condom. As he let his Alpha's words wash over him, he realized that like in everything else, DeMatteo was being cautious and giving him time to accept their true connection. That final thought caused his heart to soar and his body to relax fully, allowing that huge member to slide into his all too willing body.

"That's it, Hugh. You're doing so good, baby. Stay nice and open for me. Such a good boy," DeMatteo praised as he pushed steadily forward, not stopping until his hips were flush to Hugh's ass. Slowly, DeMatteo pulled out just an inch before he pushed back inside.

Hugh buried his face in the pillows, searing pain causing his back to arch as the thick cock shoveling inside threatened to split him in two. His lion, however, was rolled over on his back in complete submission under the alpha, not even bothering to try to ease the pain that paralyzed him.

"You okay?"

"Yeah, um, yes I'm good. I just need a minute."
Hugh's body trembled and clenched rhythmically at the
invasion.

"Fuck, Hugh, so tight." DeMatteo groaned while
digging his fingers in deep enough to leave marks, and that
sound made Hugh push his hips back a little harder.
Desperate to please his Alpha, Hugh felt his lion curl in on
itself, not willing to do anything to upset their protector.

"O… okay… I'm ready."

After his lion had absorbed all the pain of
penetration, each thrust pushed that tingle wrapping around
his spine into a flare of pleasure. Slowly he picked up the
rhythm and began to push back against his Alpha on legs
that shook. He dropped his shoulders into the mattress in an
attempt to fuck back, but it was DeMatteo that set the
quickening pace.

Hugh's mouth dropped open in a silent scream and
he struggled to breathe as the air was punched out of him
with each powerful slam of DeMatteo's hips. The pace was
perfect, stimulating in a way that slammed the slight pain
of being stretched and filled so brutally to just the right side
of blinding pleasure.

DeMatteo ~

DeMatteo tightened his grip on Hugh, nails just short of drawing blood, when he pulled back a couple of inches. His eyes were glued to where Hugh's hole was stretched obscenely around him, the skin blanched white, before shoving back in. He repeated the slow drag again and again, and each time he pushed in marginally quicker.

After what seemed like hours of steady build-up they settled into a rough rhythm, DeMatteo pushed down on Hugh's waist which caused his ass to rise higher, which also allowed DeMatteo to slide his cock deeper on every plunge.

DeMatteo had to clench his eyes shut as Hugh tightened around him. DeMatteo felt his orgasm pull his balls closer to his body, and he picked up the pace. DeMatteo knew he wouldn't last much longer as he wrapped one hand around the back of Hugh's neck and braced the other by his head to hold him still and gain leverage to hit his prostate dead on. Through it all his lion was strangely silent, having turned its back to this fake mating.

"Come on… Come on, Hugh. Come now," DeMatteo growled, hips jerking as he slammed in for the last time as he began to lose it.

DeMatteo reached between Hugh and the bed to grab ahold of his neglected cock. Hugh let out a sound that could only be called a choked off roar as his entire body tensed before he came so hard that the first spurts landed on his neck.

DeMatteo draped himself across Hugh's back, forcing them both flat as the last spasms of his orgasm spilled from him. He pulled Hugh tighter to his body as his hips continued to rock. Spent, DeMatteo sprawled uselessly on the fucked out man as they both panted while their hearts raced.

"Get off…" Hugh huffed, undoubtedly becoming uncomfortable under two hundred pounds of dead weight. DeMatteo chuckled before he reached between their bodies to grasp the condom before he pulled out and rolled off the bed.

Hugh barely regained the strength to turn his head and watch as the most perfect specimen of man he had ever encountered strolled into the bathroom. Hugh couldn't help but grin at the sight as he felt the tingles of pain he knew wouldn't last; his body already healing itself.

Chapter 6

Five years later...

"I am not interested in sending out any scent markers. Why can't you just leave this alone?"

"Look, Hugh, I know you and my brother have been together for a while, but eventually he is going to find his true mate. I just don't think you should be putting your whole life on hold for what will only ever be a temporary relationship."

"Temporary? It's been five years, Samantha! When are you going to realize that we are staying together? I am not going anywhere and neither is DeMatteo."

"This has nothing to do with me, it's…"

Hugh jumped from his seat, and whatever excuse she was starting was cut off quickly.

"Exactly! My relationship with DeMatteo has absolutely nothing to do with you. But still you feel the need to have an opinion. And what makes you think either of us even has a true mate? When was the last true mating of a gay Alpha? I'll tell you when: never! So why would your brother be any different? They all wind up taking a companion mate eventually." Hugh scowled as he stared down the Beta lioness.

Samantha stood slowly as she returned his gaze with what could only be described as disgust. She wondered if DeMatteo ever truly saw how manipulative Hugh really was. The way he tried to assume the position of Alpha Mate, weaseling his way into pride affairs. She had warned her brother many times that when he finally met his true mate, Hugh would pose a threat to their mating. But DeMatteo, for reasons she could never hope to understand, had chosen to trust Hugh.

"First, and most importantly, I could give less of a fuck about you and if you meet your mate. I am here because my brother was concerned that you were not seeking out your own true mate, so that should give you an idea of how serious he takes this 'relationship.' But you are correct, I have never seen a true mated gay Alpha. And it is true that they all take a *female* companion mate to continue their family line. But we both know that my brother will never mate someone just to breed them. In fact, he will never mate anyone that is not his true mate. And it's best you realize this now and save yourself future embarrassment."

"DeMatteo loves me! You have no idea what he wants to do with me. You have no clue what our relationship is."

"Yes, my brother cares for you. If not, he would have let me disembowel you by now. But I know my brother, and I know you will never be anything more than his favorite fuck until he meets his mate."

The knock on the door startled both shifters as they circled one another. Before either could acknowledge the visitor's presence, Carla's companion mate opened the door to Hugh's office.

"Hey, sorry to interrupt…"

"Not a problem, I was just leaving. Hugh, it would do you well to remember what I've said."

Hugh and Nick watched silently as Samantha left the room. Hugh had to take several deep breaths to push his lion down, before turning back to address the human.

"So, Nick, how can I help you today?"

Nick stood blinking at the space that Samantha had occupied for a few seconds before he seemed to remember what he had in fact come by for.

"Oh yeah. Actually, I just came down to see if you'd be interested in hanging out? I was headed to town to catch a movie. Carla is headed out with DeMatteo, so I figured we could have our own day out."

Hugh snorted at the human. He was companion mated to Carla, and yet she was still headed to another pride with DeMatteo in search of her true mate and he chose to use this time to go to the movies.

"You mean the losers left at home while their mates go out in search for someone to replace them day?" Hugh sneered dismissively.

"Umm. Well I just, you know what, never mind." Nick backpedaled. He almost ran into the sofa in his haste to leave the office.

"Fuck, Nick I didn't mean that. Just ignore me, Samantha has always had a way of pushing all of my buttons."

"Yeah, no worries. I'm just gonna let you get back to your work."

Hugh watched the human leave his office and silently kicked himself for his lack of filter. Nick had always been friendly, and Hugh really needed to make a friend of his own. He decided to make an effort to connect with someone other than his mate. Hugh ran out to catch up with the human.

"Hey, Nick! Wait up, I just need to grab my wallet."

Chapter 7

DeMatteo ~

Almost thirty years after the death of his parents
and with the pride lands secured, DeMatteo found himself
in a place he had never even considered. He had passed the
bar with flying colors and taken the position of senior
partner in his pride's law firm after Duncan Santiago's
"retirement." All in all, DeMatteo believed that he was
fulfilling his father's dying wish. But that was not what
was surprising.

"Good morning, Alpha." Hugh moaned as he
slowly opened his multicolored eyes. "Are you watching
me sleep?"

"Yes," DeMatteo answered easily as he brushed
their lips together, amazed he got to wake up with this
beautiful man each day. That feeling alone was the biggest
surprise.

DeMatteo was happier than he had been before his
parents' death. He had a thriving career and a stable pride,
and in truth, he had more than any one man could rightfully
ask for. He had Hugh, a man who gave him more love than

he ever thought he'd be given, even without a true mate bond drawing them together.

But that was DeMatteo the man. There was another consciousness just below the skin, and his lion cared for nothing but finding their true mate. Every day it grew harder to keep it from clawing its way to the surface, in search of their mate.

"Come on, my Alpha, let's get ready for the day," Hugh purred suggestively and DeMatteo was quick to follow the smaller shifter into the shower.

Hugh ~

As usual, Hugh found himself pressed against the Alpha from lips to knees the instant the soap was rinsed from his body. On any other day, Hugh was more than willing to let his Alpha worship his body and take complete control. But today he wanted to be the one watching the man he loved fall apart in his hands.

Breaking the kiss, Hugh chuckled breathlessly as he watched DeMatteo blink dazedly. Once he had the Alpha's attention, he offered a wicked grin before dropping to his knees.

"I wanna suck you off," Hugh breathed as he nuzzled into DeMatteo's groin where the scent of Alpha and lust was strongest. "Is that okay?" Hugh asked before lapping slowly against his sensitive tip.

"Fuck yes." DeMatteo's voice was so thick with need it sounded more like a growl. His hands twitched and Hugh could sense the Alpha's desire to just shove Hugh's mouth down on his cock.

Hugh wasted no time and took him in deep from the start until he felt DeMatteo give a small thrust. Pulling back, he swirled his tongue around the head before he slid back down halfway to the root. Hollowing his cheeks, Hugh made sure to steadily increase the suction as he picked up the pace.

DeMatteo hips spasmed as he fought to not slam his hips forward. If Hugh wasn't so far gone he would tease the big bad Alpha about way he whimpers, whines, and moans. But Hugh is too focused on sucking out every drop of pre-cum as it beads from the tip and coaxing as many babbled curse as he can squeeze out of the bigger man.

"Jesus, fuck! Just like that. So good, baby." DeMatteo groaned as Hugh took him to the root, his head bobbing fast and eager as his eyes welled up with tears and spit ran down his chin. Hugh upped his game by massage the heavy balls that were bouncing off his chin.

"Mmm…" Hugh moaned out around the dick in his mouth as DeMatteo began to minutely thrust. "Come on, Alpha," Hugh said after he pulled off with a wicked pop, a string of saliva spanned from his lip to the cock he had been swallowing. "I don't want you to be gentle. I want you to fuck my face."

"You sure? Don't wanna hurt you. I'm close."

"Yeah, I'm sure. Use me, Alpha." With that, Hugh slid back down as far as he could and relaxed his throat as he felt it touch. Hugh placed both hands on DeMatteo's thighs as he looked up, wordlessly begging for DeMatteo to let go and give them both what they wanted.

"Fuck!" DeMatteo swore as he looked down at his lover, totally submissive in his demands. DeMatteo finally went with his instincts and grabbed two fistfuls of hair before he gave a small thrust to no doubt gauge Hugh's reaction.

Hugh just moaned louder as DeMatteo's dick nudged just inside of his throat. DeMatteo's fingers tightened in his hair at the vibrations, and Hugh's lack of gagging encouraged him to snap his hips forward just that much quicker.

Hugh just relaxed further and breathed through his nose as he nodded slightly in reassurance and opened his mouth even wider so DeMatteo could fuck his throat.

Hugh tried to ignore the throbbing of his own cock as he focused on swallowing every time DeMatteo bottomed out.

"Goddammit, Hugh, not going to last."

DeMatteo tugged at his hair and lifted his head before he shoved it back down, setting a fast pace. Every few thrusts DeMatteo pulled him all the way off so he could paint Hugh's lips with his pre-come before forcing his face into his balls.

"That's it, Hugh. You look so good on your knees, mouth stuffed with my cock. You like that, baby?" DeMatteo asked as he dragged his cock across Hugh's lips.

Hugh immediately tried to take him back into his mouth, suckling, eager to get another taste, to have him spill down his throat. A pathetic whimper escaped as DeMatteo brutally tugged his head away from his prize.

Hugh blinked up dazedly and realized that DeMatteo was waiting for an answer.

"Yes, Alpha. I like it. I love sucking your cock."

He was rewarded with DeMatteo shoving ruthlessly back into his mouth. DeMatteo wasted no time with gentle; he fucked back into Hugh's mouth with an even more brutal pace this time. DeMatteo pushed forward until he reached the back of Hugh's throat. He paused momentarily then shoved further into his throat, until Hugh's eyes were rimmed in tears and his chin was coated with drool.

"Shit, I'm going to lose it. You ready?"

Hugh gave a choked moan in response before DeMatteo held his head in place as he slammed in a few more times before he stilled. His cock was buried so deep that the first burst seemed to bypass his tongue, before DeMatteo pulled back.

"God! Fuck! So good. Such a good boy."

DeMatteo gripped Hugh's head tight as he slammed his cock back into Hugh's throat as he continued to come. DeMatteo pulled back every so often, just enough to let him breathe as he swallowed each burst of cum.

Hugh struggled to breathe through his nose in between each impatient thrust of the powerful thighs that he clung to in a bid to keep himself from touching his dick. When he heard his Alpha's growl cut off into a desperate whimper, it had Hugh dangerously at the edge.

Hugh dutifully attempted to nurse every drop of cum his Alpha could produce, his tongue eagerly chasing every drop that had managed to escape. Hugh found his hands kneading DeMatteo's glutes; that was the only thing his lover ever denied him, but Hugh still found himself begging for that last form of intimacy.

DeMatteo ~

"Don't," DeMatteo growled much harsher than he intended. His lion bristled at what it saw as the other man's attempt to mount him.

DeMatteo knew that Hugh desperately wanted to fuck him, and even though he cared for the man deeply, that was the one thing DeMatteo had sworn he would save for his true mate.

Hugh pulled his hands back as if he'd been smacked and DeMatteo winced as he felt his lover's mood begin to sour with the sickly scent of sadness. DeMatteo quickly joined him on the shower floor before the situation became impassable.

"You know I can't, baby boy; my lion will not allow it," DeMatteo consoled as he pinned Hugh to the floor and began scenting his neck.

Hugh mewled and tipped his head back as his lover began to nuzzle and lick a path from his neck to his chest. DeMatteo paused long enough to nibble on his nipple, hard enough to pull out a yelp before he licked away the hurt.

Sucking his own fingers, DeMatteo reached down, ignoring Hugh's obscenely hard dick, and slowly massaged Hugh's hole, not pushing in, not yet, just a constant pressure, and a promise of release.

"Do you want me to fuck -" DeMatteo asked and Hugh was nodding before the question left his lips.

"Yes. Please, Alpha." Hugh moaned, voice shaky.

As he backed away DeMatteo ordered, "Get up on the bed. I want to see your pretty little hole."

Hugh scrambled to comply and almost brained DeMatteo in his haste to get back into the bedroom; he did not even stop to finish drying his skin. DeMatteo bit back a smile as he quickly dried himself before he joined the eager cub.

Walking into the room, DeMatteo almost choked at the sight of Hugh's presentation, back arched, ass up high, as he used his hands to spread himself open. DeMatteo forced himself to keep his steps slow and measured as he made his way to the bed.

"God, you are absolutely beautiful like this for me," DeMatteo said as he grabbed the half-empty bottle of lube they kept on the dresser.

He opened Hugh up carefully, never wanting to rush even when his dick was again painfully hard from the display. Gone was the timid lover DeMatteo had brought to his bed all those years ago. This was a man who knew how to get what he wanted.

"You ready?"

"God yes! Please. I am so ready," Hugh moaned as he rocked back onto the fingers scissoring inside him.

DeMatteo growled and fastened one hand around the back of his neck as he slid in with one smooth stroke. DeMatteo immediately started to fuck into him, knowing that Hugh was desperate to come after being hard for so long.

Within minutes, Hugh spilt into the sheets untouched, his passage squeezed DeMatteo to the point of pain as he continued to rut, fucking him through his orgasm. As Hugh collapsed limply against the mattress, DeMatteo was suddenly desperate to fuck his cum into him.

Still unsettled by the scene in the shower DeMatteo felt the need to reassure his lover by spilling his seed into him.

As they both settled together, boneless, DeMatteo couldn't help but wonder how long he would be able to hold onto this little piece of happiness.

Epilogue

5 years later.

"DeMatteo, I can't believe you are going to miss the gathering for a meeting."

Timothy stared at his brother's back as he pulled out his favorite gray pinstripe suit, DeMatteo just huffed in response. They had gone over this three times already this morning. It wasn't as if he could ignore his clients.

"These events happen only once every hundred years, DeMatteo, and this is going to be the largest one ever. This will be the best chance you have to find your true mate. Is this human worth taking that risk?" Timothy asked. "You know I never would have met my mate if it wasn't for the last gathering."

"Yes, Timothy, I know. Trust me, if this wasn't our biggest client, I would have just rescheduled, but I have to be there. It should be pretty quick since there is a prenuptial in place. I will go as soon as the meeting is over," DeMatteo stated more confidently than he felt.

Ever since the phone rang, he'd had an overwhelming feeling that something was about to happen. His lion restlessly paced inside his head. It was as if the fates were whispering that he needed to be in that meeting, that his life would be forever changed by it. But that wasn't something he could explain to himself, let alone anyone else.

"Anyway, Jacob will be taking my scent markings so every Alpha can take it back to his pride. If my mate is at the gathering or any of the prides, I will find him. Just like you found Kim." DeMatteo smirked. As ridiculous and outdated the process was, every unmated lion jumped at the opportunity to have their scent exchanged.

While he headed out to his car, DeMatteo set his phone's GPS for a small law firm in Seattle. He would be meeting Mr. Malone in the garage before their meeting with Mrs. Malone and the new opposing counsel.

DeMatteo stopped in the kitchen on his way to the garage to grab his briefcase and case files. Hugh looked up from the various construction floor plans spread across the counter and offered him a blinding smile.

"You headed out?" Hugh asked as he tilted his head back for a kiss.

The last few months had become increasingly strained since DeMatteo had taken to actively look for his true mate. He cared deeply for Hugh, even loved him in his own way, but DeMatteo knew they would never be in love. Not with knowing that somewhere his true mate was also waiting and looking for him.

"Yeah. I shouldn't be too long. You sure you don't want to go to the conference?" DeMatteo asked. Hugh's body visibly tensed as he twirled in his seat to look at DeMatteo, and it was hard for the Alpha in him to not see his lover's reactions as a challenge.

"Nah, I've got too much stuff to do here," Hugh answered shortly. This was starting to become par for the course, almost any conversation turning sour with only a few words.

DeMatteo had to beat back his lion's desire to force the younger male to submit. It didn't recognize Hugh as a potential mate so these outbursts were seen as direct challenges to his position. "Well if you change your mind, it's only for two days. You might like it."

Hugh narrowed his eyes, "Trying to get rid of me?" Though he tried to make the question seem playful, he completely missed the mark. Though his tone had been light and teasing, DeMatteo could sense the man's unease.

DeMatteo grabbed his chin and lifted his head until their eyes met. "Never," he said and it was true.

While DeMatteo wanted desperately to meet his true mate Hugh would always be a member of his pride. There were few things, short of death, that could sever an Alpha's connection with a pride mate. He gave Hugh another quick kiss and quickly made his way to the door before he could come up with a response. DeMatteo threw his jacket and briefcase in the car, and headed towards Seattle to meet with his client's future ex-wife, Mrs. Malone and her attorney, Mr. Sean Herr.

To Be Continued….

About the Author

Sharon Johnson is the pen name for a natural born story teller. The youngest of five, Sharon found the art of creating tales that had her parents often wondering if her adventures were real. Born and raised in New York City, Sharon spent most of her after school hours curled up with a book. An avid reader from childhood young Sharon took to expanding on her favorite stories, creating fan fictions. A former United States Marine she has a quick wit and a vocabulary that would make most sailors blush. Sharon spends most of her days as an ordinary electronics technician. If by ordinary you mean a heavily tattooed, pierced, and fiery redhead.

Sharon now resides in the beautiful Pocono Mountains with her husband, four children, two dogs, and two cats. She sets out every day to prove that you can never have too much on your plate if you love what you do. Mostly Sharon is a believer in love no matter what form you find it in. She specializes in M/M with Alpha males who are complex and flawed but are willing to fight for their HEA.

Word of mouth is vital for any author. If you enjoyed this book please leave a review where you purchased it, on Goodreads, or post it on your social media site. Sharon spends most of her nights writing but would love to hear from you.

You can email her: mail.sharonjohnson@sharonjohnsonauthor.com

You can find her on Facebook: Facebook.com/SharonJohnson1979

You can Tweet her: Twitter.com/SJohnson_Author

Visit her website: www.SharonJohnsonAuthor.com

Check her blog: http://sharonjohnsonauthor.com/blog.html

Visit her on Instagram: www.instagram.com/sharondjohnson

Sign up for Sharon's monthly newsletter. Get sneak peeks, deleted scenes, be the first to know future release dates, first glance at cover reveals, a chance to receive free ARC's, join her beta team, and so much more!

Also Available

Beyond a Reasonable Doubt

Book 1 of the Doubt Series

DeMatteo Santiago is the Alpha of one of the largest prides in North America. He is a young, successful lion shifter, surrounded by a large family and his devoted lover. By anyone's account he has more than any one man can ask for, but his lion cares of nothing except finding their mate.

An unexpected business trip pits DeMatteo and his long awaited mate on opposite sides of the courtroom. But when challenged by ex-lovers, nosey siblings, and crazy hunters, DeMatteo realizes that finding his mate was the easy part. The real question is whether they will live long enough to be together.

This release is an M/M paranormal shifter romance. This series will contain, graphic violence, graphic language, and Mpreg. What it will not be is an instant mate fairy tale, as forces set out to destroy everything and everyone.

Where Doubt Remains

Book 2 in the Doubt Series

The story continues for Alpha DeMatteo Santiago and his mate. After the nightmare of having his pregnant mate kidnapped and tortured, DeMatteo begins the seemingly impossible process of piecing together the truth. Forces against them take this time to regroup and launch an all-out attack. Lies and half-truths fall apart as the past is investigated, but it's a race against time and failure could prove to be fatal…

This release is an M/M paranormal shifter romance. This series will contain scenes of graphic violence, graphic sex, graphic language, Mpreg, and graphic birth. What it will not be is an instant mate fairy tale, as forces set out to destroy everything and everyone around him.

A League of Gentlemen

Book 1 of The Gentlemen's League series

Dominic has spent his entire life fighting and hiding. After leaving the Marine Corps, he is embarking on a new chapter in his life and cutting all ties to the man he was before.

He's in a new place with a new name. But some ugly truths from his past, truths he thought were long buried, will come back-- and these truths are refusing to be ignored.

Ladies and Gentlemen

Book 1.5 of The Gentlemen's League Series

Natasha Tsarsko is a CIA agent with a dubious past. She is second in command for a specialized unit of operatives that work in the shadows of organized crime.

She's built her career on capturing the worst kinds of criminals. In her world, getting close to the wrong person can get you killed. But what happens when someone she trusts wants her to risk it all?

Coming Soon

Only Truth Remains

Book 3 in Doubt Series

Philip Cooke is the Alpha of the Montana Wolf Pack; they have served as the head enforcers for the Joint Counsel for over a hundred years mostly because of their ability to remain neutral. But when a call from Richard Santiago, Alpha Apex of all shifters in North America, summons him to hunt down a rogue lion, his options of remaining neutral disappear.

Once in Seattle, Philip meets Alpha Mate Sean and Alpha DeMatteo Santiago, nephew of the Alpha Apex and target of the rogue lion's affections. The case takes a bizarre turn when the rogue lion is killed in a failed attack, but his death leaves more questions than answers. Talk of the true mated gay Alpha had reached the pack lands, but Philip had dismissed the talks as mere rumors. Now with the undeniable evidence all around him, Phillip has to reevaluate all he has ever known and sacrificed.

When all the players are identified, one of the hunters appear to be the lost offspring of one of his own. Soon Phillip will learn that his pack is more deeply involved in this plot than anyone had ever realized, and choices made long ago have explosive consequences today. The death toll rises, but the case is far from over. In fact, it seems to be headed even closer to home.

Coming Soon

No Man Left Behind

Book 2 in The Gentlemen's League Series

The trail heats up in the search for the mole hiding within the Hive, but in the game of espionage there is always another game being played just below the surface. New passions heat up and take center stage as we continue Dominic's journey to a new life.

Up and until a few months ago, Samuel Wright has never spent any significant time thinking about his love life. Although to be fair, few of his conquests spanned beyond a couple of sweaty encounters, and until very recently, he had never seen a need for more. Men, women, and everything in between, Samuel liked to think of his bed as a sexual United Nations. There was no reason to limit his options.

Well, that was true until a certain spook joined their team...

www.ingramcontent.com/pod-product-compliance
Lightning Source LLC
Chambersburg PA
CBHW070501130626
46555CB00003B/1100